Smile, Please!

Poems by Tony Bradman

Illustrated by Jean Baylis

PUFFIN BOOKS

PUFFIN BOOKS

Published by the Penguin Group
Penguin Books Ltd, 27 Wrights Lane, London W8 5TZ, England
Penguin Books USA Inc., 375 Hudson Street, New York, New York 10014, USA
Penguin Books Australia Ltd, Ringwood, Victoria, Australia
Penguin Books Canada Ltd, 10 Alcorn Avenue, Toronto, Ontario, Canada M4V 3B2
Penguin Books (NZ) Ltd, 182–190 Wairau Road, Auckland 10, New Zealand

Penguin Books Ltd, Registered Offices: Harmondsworth, Middlesex, England

First published by Viking Kestrel 1987
Published in Puffin Books 1989
3 5 7 9 10 8 6 4

Printed in England by Clays Ltd, St Ives plc
Filmset in Century Schoolbook

FOR SALLY –

the best so far, for the best always

Contents

Smile, Please!

Look in the camera,
It's time for a snap,
Don't look too funny –
The camera might crack!

Time to say jelly,
Time to say cheese,
Time for my dad
To say – 'Smile, please!'

Never a Dull Moment

If you like to keep lively,
If you hate being bored,
Just come down to our house
And knock on the door.

It's the noisiest house
In the whole of our town,
There's doors always slamming
And things falling down.

There's my dad, who keeps shouting,
And my mum, who breaks things,
The baby (who'll bite you!)
And our dog running rings.

There's my sister the screamer
And my brother who roars,
And a grandpa who's stone deaf
(He's the one who slams doors).

So come down to our house,
You don't need the address,
You'll hear it ten miles away
And the outside's a mess.

You won't mind the racket,
You'll just love the din –
For there's never a dull moment
In the house *we* live in!

TEA

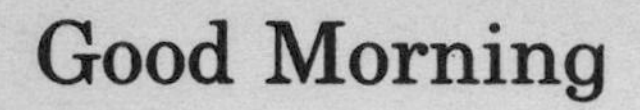

Good Morning

In the mirror
I can see
A face I know –
It could be me!

Here's a toothbrush
And some paste
For the teeth
In that face

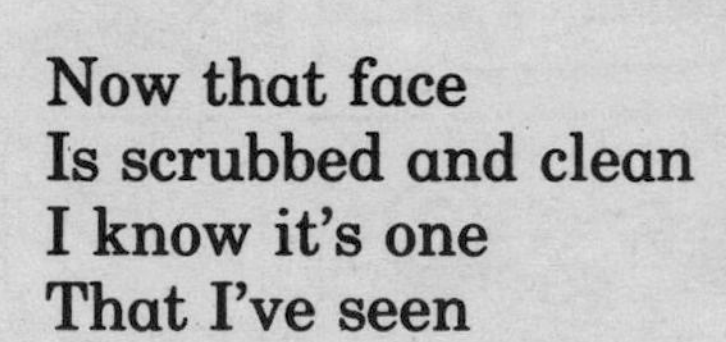

Now that face
Is scrubbed and clean
I know it's one
That I've seen

In the mirror
Clean and yawning
That *is* my face
Good morning!

Food

I like breakfast
I like tea
I like putting
Food in me

I like cornflakes
I like toast
But I like my egg
The most

Slice the top off
Poke about
Pull the dripping
Yolk right out

I like breakfast
I like tea
I love putting
Food in me

Only The Lonely

I've never had
A room of my own
I've never been able
To sit alone
And read or think
Or laze about
Alone in the quiet

I'm only alone
When I go

Out

Boots

When the rain is raining,
When it's raining on the street,
I'm glad I've got my boots on,
My boots upon my feet.

For when the rain is raining,
I can splash and I can stamp,
And while I've got my boots on
My feet will not get damp.

And when the rain is raining,
I've got my little brolly;
I'll keep it up above my head
And stay quite dry and jolly.

But when the rain is pouring,
When it comes down very fast,
I think we'd better stay in –
Until the storm is past!

Paul's Ball

My name's Paul
And I'm kicking my ball
Against the wall

Wall	Paul	Paul
Ball	Ball	Paul
Wall	Wall	Ball
Ball	Paul	Wall
Paul	Ball	Paul

P-ping	Whackety-whack
P-Paul	Thwackety-ping
P-ping	Kick it back
P-Paul	Kick that thing

Right foot
Left foot
Left foot
Left foot
Left foot right
Kick it all day
Kick it all night

Lean back
Give it a ...

'PAUL! YOUR DINNER'S READY!'

... whack!

Ball Paul
Ball wall
Paul

Indoors

That's all

Dinner Time

I make a house
Under our table,
And I play there
Whenever I'm able.

I've got a cooker,
And some plates –
Teddy's hungry
And he won't wait.

I've got a telephone
And some books –
Sit right down
And take a look!

Now it's tea-time,
Mum says stop –
My dinner's waiting
On the table top!

The Gerbil

'Can we have a gerbil, mum?'
'We can't,' is what mum said.
'I'm sorry, love,' she added,
'I'm having a baby, instead.'

'I'd rather have a gerbil, mum,
I'd like a pet,' I said.
But what I'll get is a baby,
With a face all screaming and red.

'I'll tell you what,' said mother,
'I'll tell you what we'll do.
If you help me with the baby,
You can have a gerbil, too.'

I got the gerbil I wanted,
And I help mum every day.
The baby isn't too bad –
But the gerbil's quieter, I'd say.

Bonk...Owww!

My name's Tracey
And I'm always

Bonk...Owww!

Falling over.

Sometimes I'm just
Walking along when

Bonk...Owww!

I find myself
Falling over.

I'm covered in
Bruises and grazes

And when I'm not

Bonk...Owww!

Falling over

I bump into

CRASH...TINKLE

Things and knock
Them over.

My mum says
I've got two

Bonk...Owww!

Left feet but
I don't think I have.

Falling over's
Not much fun

And my dad says
It's just a stage I'm

Bonk...Owww!

Going through...

But how will I
Get through it if I'm

Bonk...Owww!
CRASH...TINKLE, TINKLE...

Always

Falling

Over?

All On My Own

My dad says I'm getting big
And I can do so much now
All on my own

I can get washed and brush
My teeth and get dressed now
All on my own

I can write my own name
And lots of other words too
All on my own

I'm on level three readers
And I can almost read now
All on my own

Sometimes I have to read
To Miss Bottomley
All on my own

When I come home from school
I make myself a drink
All on my own

At dinner time mum
Lets me lay the table
All on my own

I have a bedroom where
Sometimes I can go to be
All on my own

At night I lie in my bed
And listen to the telly downstairs
All on my own

I listen for their voices
And I fall asleep
All on my own

It's nice to know they're close
And I'm not really
All on my own

The Fish

I am a little fishy
I live down in the sea
I swim around
Without a sound

I like being me

Down to Earth

I climbed a tree,
I got too high,
My dad said I could
Touch the sky.

But I fell down,
And bumped my head.
So I think I'll stick
To the ground instead.

Sisters

You're not coming into my room.
  – I am.
No you're not.
  – I am.
Oh no you're not.
  – Why can't I come in?
I don't want you to.
  – Why don't you want me to?
I just don't want you to.
  – I'm coming in.
YOU'RE NOT!
  – I AM, I AM!
MUM! DAD!

– All right, all right.
Nah Nah Nee Nah Nah!
– Do you know what?
What?
– I didn't want to come in anyway.
?
– I really didn't.
Oh yes you did.
– I didn't.
Did.
– Didn't.
Did, did…
– Didn't, didn't, didn't…

One Two Three Four

One two three four
Start by playing on the floor

Five six seven eight
Riding my bike right up to the gate

Nine ten eleven twelve
In the garden dig and delve

Twelve eleven ten nine
Back indoors it's dinner time

Eight seven six five
In my bath I splash and dive

Four three two one
Into my bed the day is done

Another Hour

Please, can I stay up late tonight?
    It's only half past seven.
I'd really like to watch TV,
My friends all watch much more than me
And there's a programme that I've *got* to see –
    Another hour would be heaven!

Please, can I stay up late tonight?
    It's only half past eight.
It really would be such a bore
To go upstairs and close my door,
The next thing on is what my friends adore –
    And sleeping's what I hate!

Please, can I stay up late tonight?
    It's only half past nine.
This programme's really got me going,
The hero's trapped inside a crashing Boeing,
Will he be saved? There's just no way of knowing –
    We really need more time!

Please, can I stay up late tonight?
    It's only half past...CLICK
What have you done? It isn't fair!
You've left that programme in mid-air...
All right, all right, I'm half way up the stairs!
    But it's still a rotten trick!

Please...can you stay with me tonight?
It's only half past eleven.
My heart is pounding...pound, pound, pound,
I'm frightened now by every sound,
My mind is going round and round and round...
Some sleep would just be...heaven!

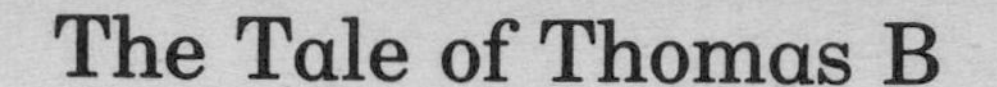

The Tale of Thomas B

This is the tale of Thomas B,
Who left home today at half past three,
He said that he was going to sea,
To be a salty sailor.

It wasn't very long before
Young Thomas B came to the shore,
Where he saw ships and sea galore,
And lots of salty sailors.

Thomas joined up and off he sailed,
But soon his ship was in a gale,
And poor young Thomas turned quite pale,
A pale and salty sailor.

Thomas came home, he left the sea,
'The sea,' he said, 'is not for me.'
And that is why young Thomas B...
Is *not* a salty sailor.

Everything Will Be All Right

I'd had a really dreadful day,
   Nothing would go right;
I failed a test and got told off,
   Then got into a fight.

I fell down in the playground
   Where I lost my special rubber,
And by the time that I got home
   All I could do was blubber.

My little brother bit me
   And I spilt my drink at tea...
Why, oh why I wondered,
   Is this happening to me?

Later, dad came to my room,
   And kissed me on my head.
He put his hand upon my hair,
   And this is what he said:

'Life is sometimes difficult,
   It's sometimes a real pain,
But something's bound to pop up, love,
   To make you laugh again.

'So close your eyes now, and forget
  That everything's gone wrong,
I promise you that in a while
  You'll laugh both loud and long.'

And can you guess what happened next?
  As dad went to the door,
He tripped and flew across the room
  And crashed down on the floor.

I laughed, I giggled, and dad said;
  'I hear you've changed your tune...
But when I said you'd cheer up,
  I didn't mean so *soon*.'

Helper

I'm a little helper,
I like to tidy up,
I help dad do the dishes –
Whoops, there goes a cup.

I'm a little helper,
I like to dust and clean,
I help dad do the hoovering –
I've got my own machine!

I'm a little helper,
I like to dig and weed,
I help dad in the garden –
I'm the only help he needs!

I'm a little helper,
I like to do my room,
Dad says I should do it now –
I'll get around to it soon!

The Fugitive

My mum told me off today.
So I thought – I'll run away.

I didn't really get too far.
I don't like walking but I've got no car.

If my mum tells me off tomorrow...
A car is the first thing that I'll borrow.

The Bear Facts

I knew a bear
Who ate an éclair.
He reached out a paw
And ate one more.
He said: 'I do declare,
I'll give up honey
And spend my money
On things less runny:
I love éclairs,
So there.'

Grandma Mabel

Grandma Mabel's
Nice and jolly,
Gives me cakes
And sticky lollies.

Grandma Mabel
Baked a cake;
I ate the lot,
Got tummy ache.

Grandma Mabel
Said to me:
I'll boil the kettle,
Make some tea.

Grandma Mabel's
Nice to me,
Cakes and smiles
And love for tea.

Grandpa John

Grandpa John
Is nice to me;
Sits me on his
Bony knees.

Tickles my chin,
Tweaks my nose,
Tells me I'm his
Little rose.

Grandpa John
Gives me some money,
Tells me I'm
His little honey.

Reads me stories,
Sings me songs;
Tells me I'm
Where I belong.

Bubble Gum

I like to
Chomp, chomp
Slurp, chomp
Chew bubble
POP!
Gum but my mum says
Chomp, chomp
Slurp, chomp
It's a disgusting
POP!
Habit

I like to
Chomp, chomp
Slurp, chomp
Chew bubble
POP!
Gum but my mum says
Chomp, chomp
Slurp, chomp
One day I'll get in
POP!
Trouble

I like to
Chomp, chomp
Slurp, chomp
Chew bubble
POP!
Gum but my mum says
Chomp, chomp
Slurp, chomp
I look like
POP!
A rabbit

I like to
Chomp, chomp
Slurp, chomp
Chew bubble
POP!
Gum but my mum says
Chomp, chomp
Slurp, chomp
I'll blow too big
POP!
A bubble

I like to
Chomp, chomp
Slurp, chomp
Chew bubble
POP!
Gum but my mum says
Chomp, chomp
Slurp, chomp
I'll be swallowed up
POP!
Inside

I like to
Push, push
Poke, push
Chew bubble
– ?
Gum but can you hear me
Poke, poke
Push, poke
– ?

Outside?

At the Park

I don't want to go out,
I don't want to play,
It's cold and it's windy –
It's a horrible day.

I don't like the park,
And I don't like the swings.
I'll just sit on the bench
And ignore everything.

I'll sulk and I'll pout,
I'll hide in my scarf,
I'll pull down my hat –
And I'll scream if you laugh!

But hold on a minute…
That see-saw looks fun!
The clouds are all going,
And here comes the sun…

Oh I'll swing on the swings,
I'll run round and play.
I'm so glad we came, mum –
Can we stay here all day?

Kiss Kiss

Kiss one, kiss two,
I love you

Kiss three, kiss four,
Do you want some more?

Kiss five, kiss six,
Kiss me quick!

Kiss seven, kiss eight,
Let's not wait

Kiss nine, kiss ten –
To start again!

Liar

I'm a liar
Everything I say is
A lie
Everything
Which means
That when I say
I'm a liar
I'm lying
So I must be telling
The truth

If I'm telling
The truth
I'm a liar
Everything I say is
A lie
Everything
Which means
That when I say
I'm a liar
I'm lying

So I must be telling
The truth

But I'm a liar
(Oh, forget it)

Ibble Obble

I once met an alien
Who said this to me:

Ibble Obble
Bibble Bobble
Bobble Bibble
Ip

Dibble Dobble
Zing bang bop
Bibble Bibble
Zip

Zibble zabble
I like scrabble
Dibble wibble
Dip

Ibble obble
Bibble bobble
Dibble nibble
Ip?

And I simply had to agree

Here Comes the Wind

Whoooooooooo...
SSSSSSssssss...
Swissshhhhhh...

Here comes the wind...
It's blowing and blowing
And blowing and growing,
It's howling and yowling,
Still roaring and pouring
From over the hill...

I CAN'T STAND STILL...

The wind's going to blow me

OVER THAT HILL...

Hold hard, in the yard,
Fight with my might, fight
That wind all night...
Puff and pant,
Puff and blow...

I'M STARTING TO GO...

Ooooooohhhhhh...
I'M GONE

CAN'T HOLD
ON

SO

LONG

GOODBYEEEEEEEEEEEEEEEeeeeee...

Whoooooooooo...
SSSSSSsssssss...
Swissshhhhhhh...

A Fantastic Poem

This is going to be
A fantastic poem when I get
Round to writing it;

It's got a story
That's gory
With bloodthirsty villains
(Named Cyril and Dylan)
It's got chases
And maces and maidens in braces
(In braces?)
It's got silver and gold
And adventurers bold
Dragons that fly
Over mountains so high
You don't run out of mountain
You just run out of sky

It's got dwarfs by the dozen
And features Kevin
(He's my cousin)
And axes and taxes
(Taxes?)
And rivers of blood
And a one-legged knight
Who flounders in mud
And something rotten
That I've forgotten

This is going to be
A fantastic poem when I get
Round to writing it;
But at the moment
I'm too busy
Fighting it

My Mum's a Dinner Lady

My mum's a dinner lady,
She helps out at my school;
My teacher says she's wonderful
And that she's no one's fool.

My mum's a dinner lady,
She helps us with our lunches;
She wipes the infants' noses
And she sorts out Sarah's bunches.

My mum's a dinner lady,
She wears an overall,
She picks us up and soothes us
If ever we should fall.

My mum's a dinner lady,
She makes me really proud;
But I must never call her *mum*
(That's simply not allowed!)

My mum's a dinner lady,
And when we're both at home,
I'm really lucky 'cos I've got...
A dinner lady of my own!

Sometimes

Sometimes

When I'm sitting in class
I look out of the window
To watch the clouds pass

The clouds
                are high
Up in
                the sky

And it's always then
Mrs Bottomley asks me why
I'm not looking at my book

Again

Bullrod the Bulldog

I'm Bullrod the Bulldog,
I'm short and I'm fat,
I'm mean and I'm nasty –
Now how about that?

I snarl and I'm vicious,
I'm really quite mean,
I snap at the postman –
He always turns green.

But deep down inside me,
I'm really quite nice –
I might eat your cat,
But I'd never eat mice.

I might eat your mother,
But I'd leave you your dad.
Now how can a dog like
That be all bad?

But people don't like me,
I know it, I do –
But if I come round to your house,
You'll like me – WON'T YOU?

The Fly

Zzzzzzzzzzzzzz...

There's a fly inside my bedroom,
It's driving me insane;
It's buzzing round my wardrobe,
It's on the windowpane...

It's flying round the lampshade,
It's coming very close.
It's landed on my pillow...
It's walking on my nose!

It's looking in my eyeball,
Phew! It's flying off again!
It's walking on the ceiling,
It's driving me insane!

It's buzzing and it's buzzing,
It's coming near again,
I'll never, ever, get to sleep.
That fly is such a pain!

It's buzzing round the bedpost,
It's walking on the floor...
It's flying round my toys and, yes!
It's buzzing out the door.

The fly's buzzed off and left me,
So now I'll close my eyes...
But wait...do I hear buzzing?
It's back, surprise, surprise!

Zzzzzzzzzzzzzzz...

Starter

Hi!
I'm cousin Art,
And I like to start
A new thing every day.
But I never finish anything;
At least that's what...they...

The Rat

I knew a rat
Who once ate a cat.

It gave him a pain;
He won't do it again.

The Class Outing

Today's our class outing,
We're going to see
A castle that's ancient
With Miss Bottomley.

We're all in the coach now,
We're bowling along,
And Miss Bottomley says
That we've got to sing songs.

But Emma's been naughty,
And Neil has been sick...
We're here at the castle,
So let's get out quick.

Miss Bottomley says that
We've got to walk round
The outside to see all
The walls from the ground.

Now Sarah's gone missing,
And Lee's lost his lunch,
And Paul's dropped his glasses,
Look out! Tinkle, crunch...

Neil didn't look well,
Miss Bottomley said,
And then he was sick
When she patted his head.

We're inside the castle,
It looks lots of fun,
But is that a cloud
Creeping over the sun?

Miss Bottomley talked
To a man by some stairs,
Who said the museum
Was closed for repairs.

We all trooped outside
And it started to rain.
Miss Bottomley said
She'd not come here again.

We're back in the coach,
And we're bowling along,
And Miss Bottomley says
That we mustn't sing songs.

She sat Neil beside her,
Right next to the door,
And when we arrived...
He was sick on the floor.

Oh wasn't it thrilling?
Wasn't it fun?
We all loved our outing –
Well, not everyone!

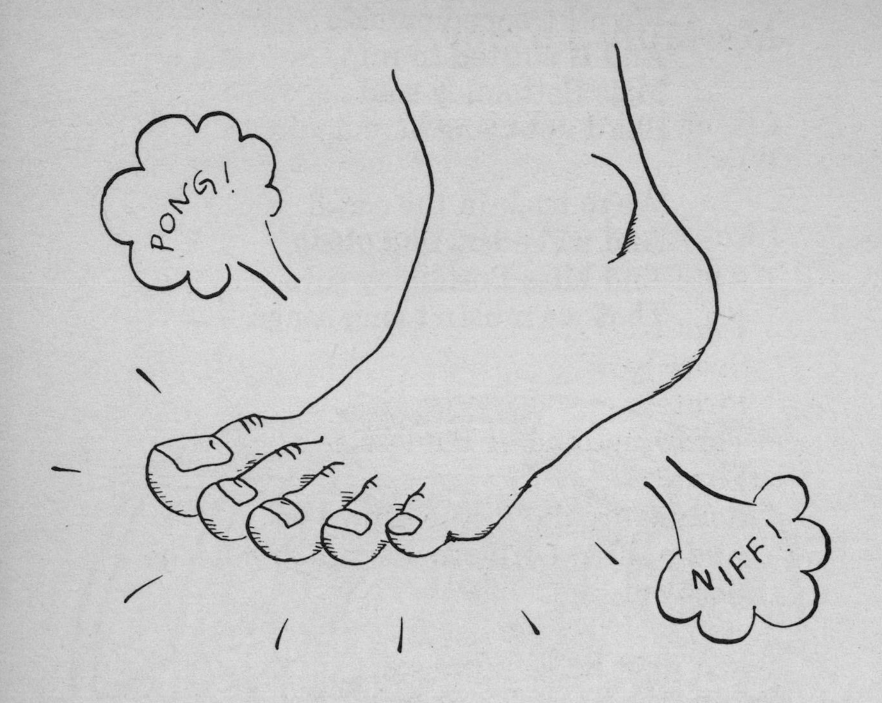

Foot Note

I'll tell you a secret
You mustn't repeat,
A secret about
My best friend's…feet.
I'm sorry to say
That my friend Ray's
Got feet that smell.
Oh, please don't tell –
He's a very good friend.
But his feet are…
the end.

My Mum's a Spy

I think my mum's a spy.
Why?

I was round at Paul's, playing.
We played:

Pirates
Space war
Pirates
Throwing mud at Paul's sister
Pirates
Rolling around in the dirt
And pulling each other through a hedge –
Backwards

When I got home mum said:
You look like you've been
Pulled through a hedge –

Backwards

Summer

When the sun gets out of bed
And lays his warm hand on my head
I wake up smiling from ear to ear
Because I know the summer's here

Rise and Shine

The sun jumped in my window,
And what did he have to say?
'Come on, wake up you sleepy head –
It's a beautiful, beautiful day!'

Chase Me

Chase me, mother,
Chase me, dad,
Whether I'm good
Or whether I'm bad.

Chase me, chase me,
Round the chairs,
Round the hall
And up the stairs.

Chase me, chase me,
Here and there,
Round the house
And anywhere.

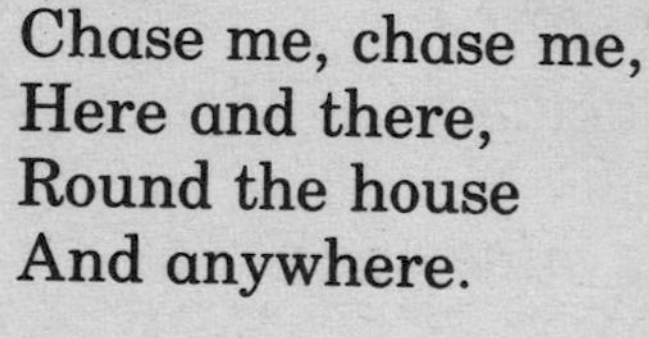

Chase me once
And chase me twice,
Being chased
Is really nice!

The Bike

This bike was bought
For my cousin, Mark;
He once fell off it
In the park.

But now it's mine.

Then it belonged
To his little sister;
She said the saddle
Gave her a blister.

And now it's mine.

Their little brother
Had it then;
And he fell off it
Again and again.

But now it's mine.

My big sister
Was next in line
And she stayed on it
All the time.

And now it's mine.

Then my brother
(Whose name is Mike)
Was the next to get
That bike.

But now it's mine.

This bike is old,
And covered in grime,
It's battered and rusty,
But to me it's fine...

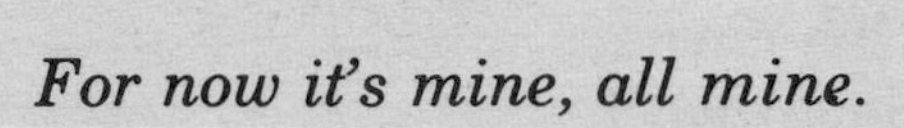

For now it's mine, all mine.

Whee!

Whee! Down the path
My bike flying fast
Wheels spinning round
Over the ground

Whoops! On the grass
I've flown too fast
I'm spinning round
Bump on the ground

A Corner of Magic

There's a park near our house
With the usual park things;
Lots of dogs, mums with babies,
A roundabout and swings.

It's scruffy, and it's dirty,
And I don't like it much;
The roundabout's squeaky
And cold to the touch.

But down in the corner,
By a tumbledown wall,
There's some trees and some bushes
Where I once lost a ball.

It was quiet and gloomy,
It was dark, it was cold,
And it felt like a place
That was creepy and old.

It felt like a forest
Full of powerful things...
Where a prince might have searched
For a magical ring,

Where a witch fought a wizard,
Where a battle took place,
Where a princess and a pauper
Once hid in disgrace...

I duddered, I shivered,
I felt very cold,
As I thought of the stories
Those trees could have told.

I turned and I ran out,
To people and light,
And my dad said I looked like
I'd had a real fright.

In the heart of the city,
In that scruffy old park,
There's a corner of magic,
Of mystery and dark.

We sometimes go back there,
And I play on the swings;
But I'll leave my lost ball
To those magical things...

At the Seaside

The day we went down to the seaside
Was a day when we had such fun,
I paddled in the cold wet sea
And played in the warm summer sun.

I dug a big hole and buried
My dad very deep in the sand,
We covered up every bit of him –
Except for his head and his hands.

I had a lovely cold lolly,
I went for a long donkey ride,
I found a sea shell and listened
To the whispering sea inside.

I built a great huge castle,
And my mum dug out a big moat,
Then we had a neat game of pirates,
And I sailed my little blue boat.

And when it was time to pack up,
To say goodbye to the sea,
I wasn't too sad because I had
My shell to take home with me.

Sticky Licky

In the summer,
When it's sunny,
Eating ice-cream
Can be funny.

Ice-cream melts
And drips so fast
It's quite hard
To make it last.

It's so lovely,
Sweet and licky,
But when it drips,
You get sticky.

I get ice-cream
On my clothes,
In my hair
And up my nose.

My dad says
I should eat less;
Ice-cream plus me
Equals – mess!

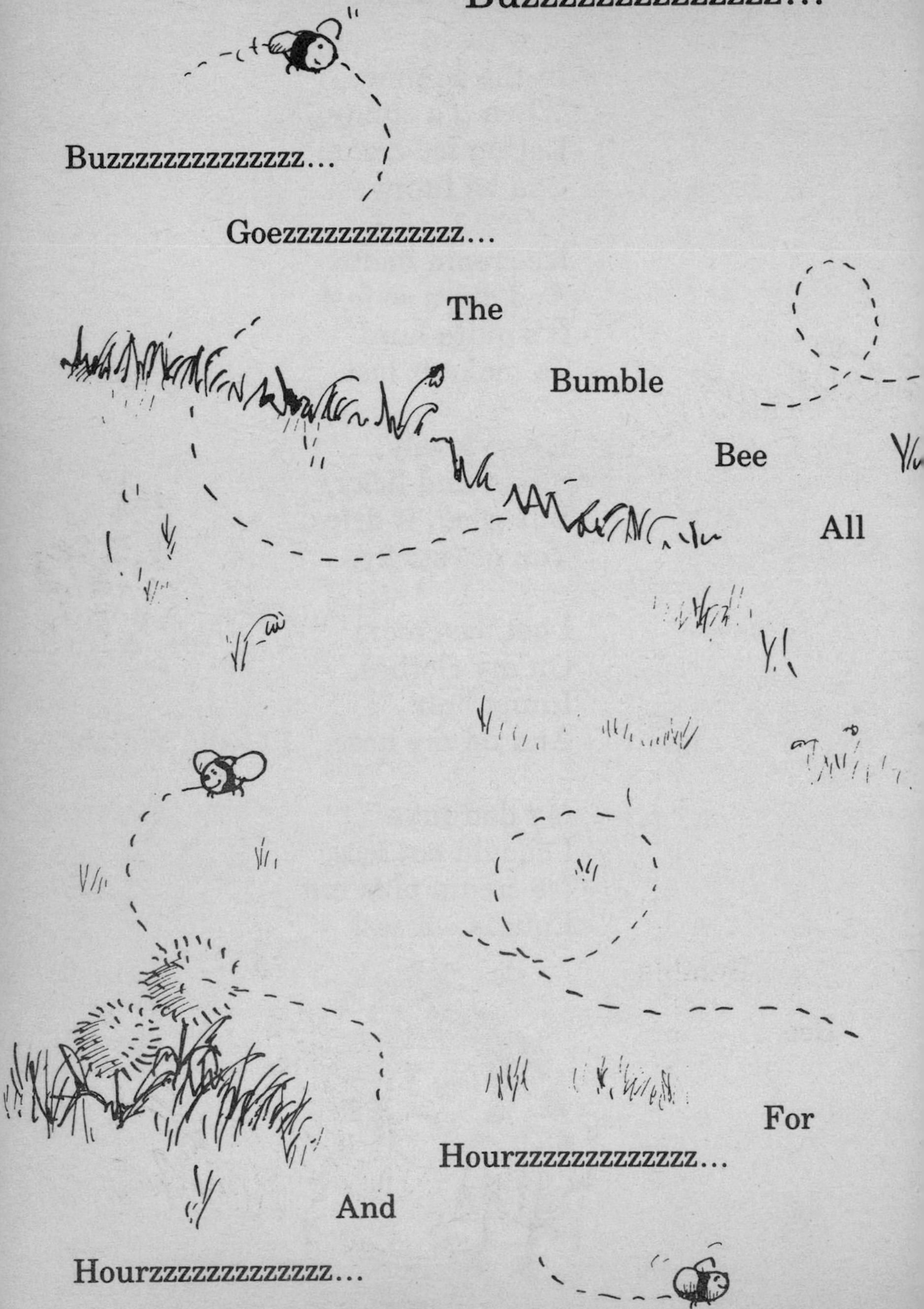

Buzzzzzzzzzzzzzzz...

Buzzzzzzzzzzzzzzz...

Goezzzzzzzzzzzzzz...

The

Bumble

Bee

All

For

Hourzzzzzzzzzzzzzz...

And

Hourzzzzzzzzzzzzzz...

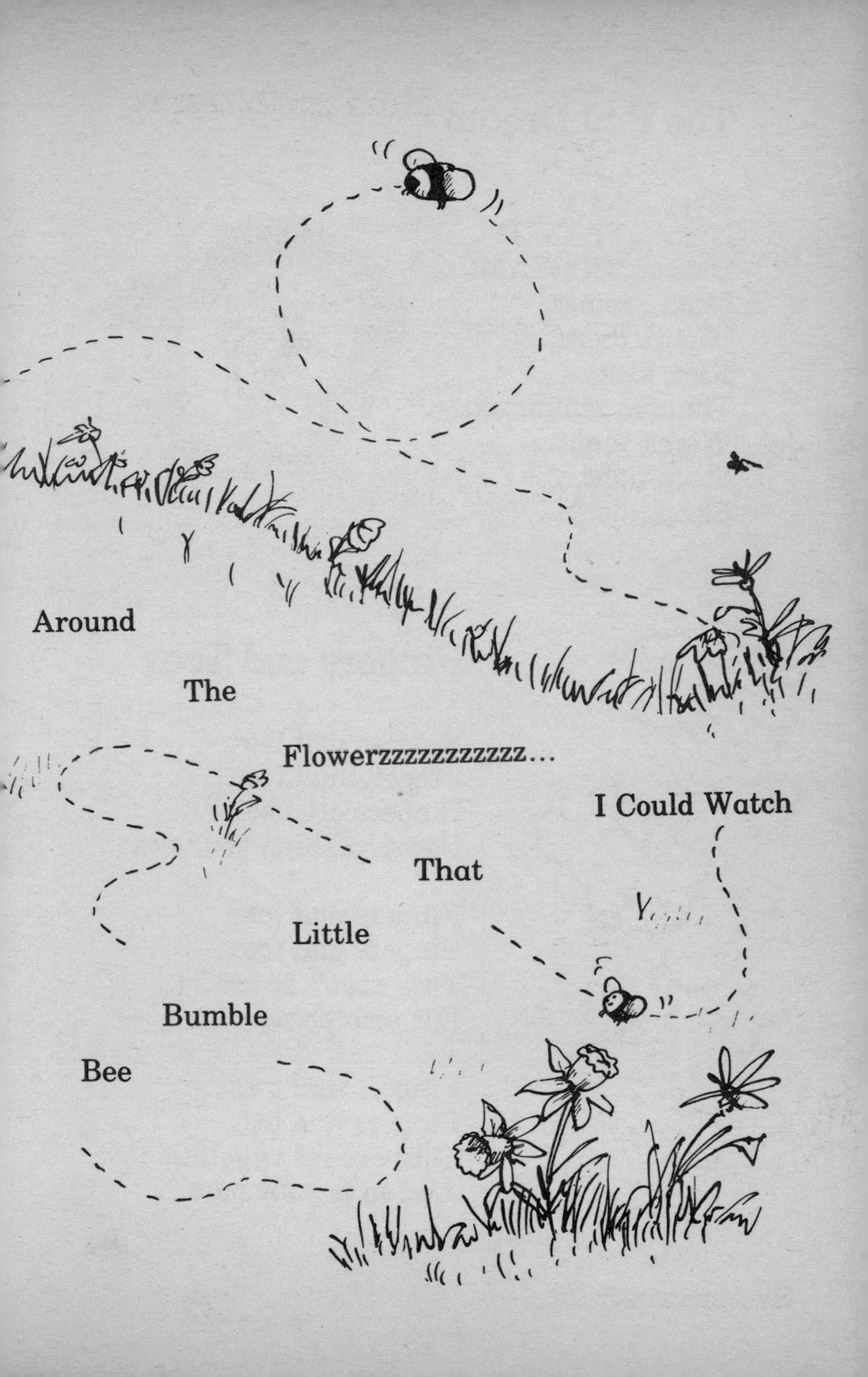
Around
The
Flowerzzzzzzzzzzz...
I Could Watch
That
Little
Bumble
Bee

The Bad Dream

Sleep…deep.
Night…FRIGHT!
Dream…SCREAM!
Mum…comes.
'There, there…'
Kiss, kiss…
Thumb…mmmmm.
'Night, night…
Sleep tight…'
Sleep…deep…

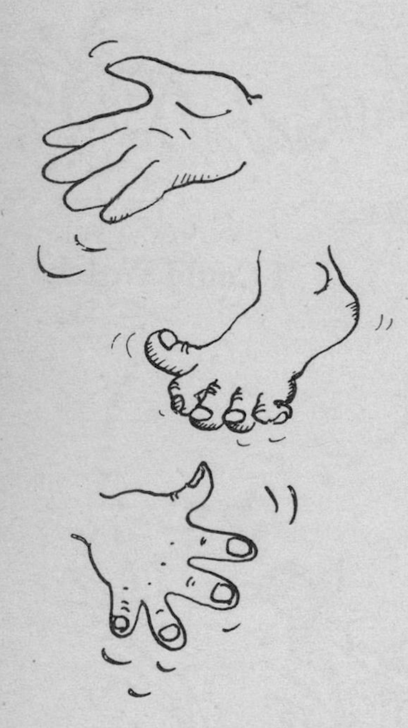

Fingers and Toes

Fingers and toes
Fingers and toes
Fingers are useful
For scratching your nose

Fingers and toes
Fingers and toes
Toes aren't so useful
For scratching your nose

Fingers and toes
Fingers and toes
Toes are for wiggling
And so is your nose

Rainy Days

When it rains
And we're indoors
We spread our toys
Out on the floor

Draw some pictures
Sing some songs
Drive dad mad
All day long

But when it's sunny
Out we run
To play our games
In the sun

Out in the park
Playing hide-and-seek –
Ssh, let dad doze off,
Let dad sleep!

I Am The Bouncing Helen

My name is Helen

Boing

I'm five and
I like to bounce

Boing
Boing

I bounce
bounce
bounce

Boing
Boing

My mum says

Boing

I'm driving her mad
With my

Boing
Boing

Bouncing

She says

Boing

I'm like a little

Bouncing rubber ball

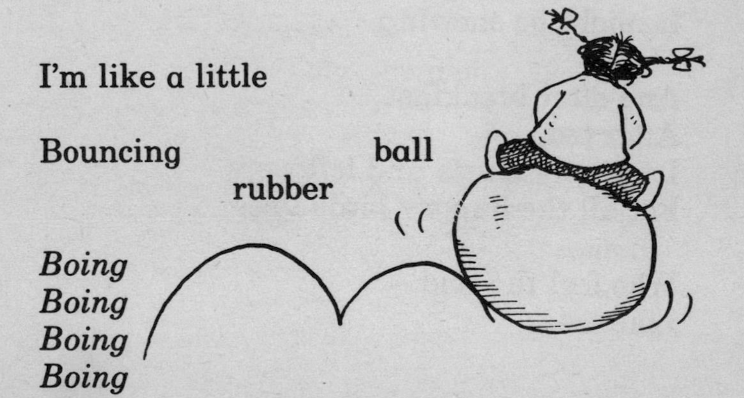

Boing
Boing
Boing
Boing

Autumn

The streets are full of autumn leaves.
I crunch and kick them
With my feet.

The wind is whistling
And it's chasing
Autumn leaves along the street.

The trees are bare
And nothing's growing.
Winter's coming and soon
It might be snowing

And after breakfast,
After tea,
I save my crusts and leftovers
For all the hungry birds I see;

Who feel the cold –
Like me.

What I Like

I like watching telly,
I like to have fun,
I like playing outside
And I love to run.

But there's one thing I love,
That I really adore –
I love reading books
And I've got to have more!

I like eating lollies
And hate them to end,
I like doing nothing
When I'm with my friends.

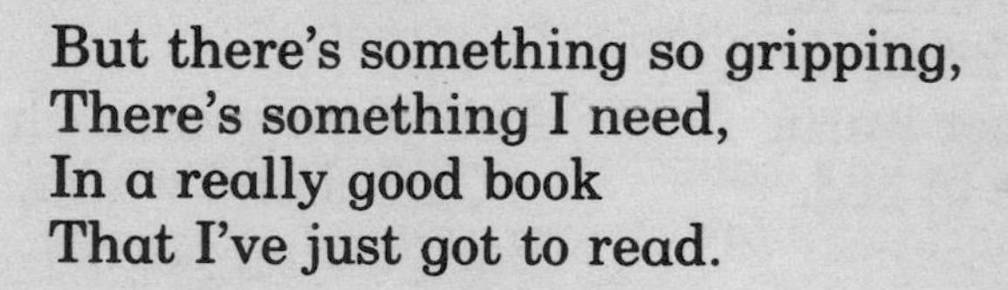

But there's something so gripping,
There's something I need,
In a really good book
That I've just got to read.

I like being awkward,
And I love to laugh,
I love eating burgers
And hate having baths.

But here's one thing that's greater,
Come inside, take a look;
There's nothing quite like
A really good book!

Purring

When my cat sleeps
Curled up in a ball,
You can't really see
Her head at all.

A furry circle,
Curled around,
Sleeping softly
With a purring sound.

She looks funny,
Does our cat,
Like a furry,
Purring hat.

I'd like to wear her
On my head,
Or have her warm
My toes in bed.

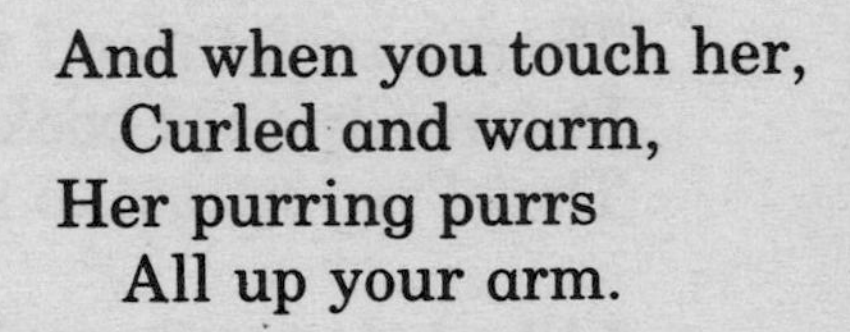

And when you touch her,
Curled and warm,
Her purring purrs
All up your arm.

But then she hears
A sudden sound
And she's no longer
Curled around;

She's not sleeping,
Softly there…
She's gone – but left
Some purring air.

You Can't Win

Sometimes
When I say
'Roll on Christmas!'
In June, or
'Can I have a new bike
For Christmas?'
In September
My dad says:
'Don't start
Talking about Christmas
Yet, it's ages away!'

And then when
It's my sister's
Birthday and I'm
Fed up
Because it isn't
Mine,
My dad says:
'Cheer up! It's
October – soon be
Christmas!'

The Name Game

Paula Brown
Has very blue eyes
And very white hair

Everyone calls her Paula

James Black
Is very pale and white
And has freckles everywhere

Everyone calls him Jim

Sarah White
Is black and her eyes
Are very brown

Everyone calls her Sarah

Peter Green's
Pale pink except for his knees
Which are dirty because he's always falling down

Everyone calls him Pete

I'm Paul Gray
And I'm pale and pink but people
Say my hair is red

Everyone calls me Ginger

I wish
They wouldn't call me Ginger
And use my proper name instead

Everyone could call me Paul –
That's all

Grandad

My Grandad has big ears
And a big nose.
He has very white hair
And very strange-looking
Little toes.
My Grandad drives his
car very fast…
ZOOOOOOMMMMMMMM…
That's him, going past.

My Grandad has a wart
On his chin
And a smile so big
You feel you could fall in
To it.
My Grandad drives his
car very fast…
ZOOOOOOMMMMMMMM…
That's him, going past.

My Grandad likes to dig
And weed in his garden
All day long.
When he spills something
At the table he says:
I do beg your pardon.
My Grandad drives his
car very fast…
ZOOOOOOOMMMMMMMM…
That's him, going past.

My Grandad's tall,
And very thin,
And everyone says
I look like him.
But I haven't got a wart
On my chin...
My Grandad drives his
car *very* fast...
ZOOOOOOOMMMMMMMM...
Toot! Toot!
Squeeeeeal...Zoom, Zoom,
ZOOOOOOOMMMMMMMM...
That's him, going past.

Tellyscare

Sometimes I don't like the scary bits on the telly,
When there's evil aliens in big silver wellies,
When there's monsters and blood
And my heart's going thud
And my knees are just turning to jelly.

I close my eyes tight or run off and hide,
Until the monsters who are right there inside
The telly have gone
Or they've been jumped upon
By a hero who's strong, tall and wide.

The only trouble is that I've just got to know
What horrors are happening, so even although
I'm really so scared
I just wouldn't dare
To turn off the telly, oh no.

I'm a Tree

Autumn leaves,
In the breeze
Falling down
On the ground.

On my knees
In the leaves,
Rolling round
On the ground.

Look at me –
I'm a tree,
Leaves all brown
And falling down!

Two Lists

I'm going out now
To the shops for my dad

I've got two lists
One of things to buy

Carrots
Peas
Bread
An apple pie

One of things to remember:

Don't talk to strangers
Go straight there
Be careful crossing the roads
Don't talk to strangers
Come straight back
Don't lose the money
Don't talk to strangers
Don't get lost
Don't forget the change

And Tommy...

Yes, dad?

Don't talk to strangers

I'm back now from going
To the shops for my dad

I didn't talk to strangers
I went straight there
I was careful crossing the roads
I didn't talk to strangers
I came straight back
I didn't lose the money
I didn't talk to strangers
I didn't get lost
I didn't forget the change
And...I didn't talk to strangers

So what did you forget?
Dad said

The carrots
The peas
The apple pie
And...

Yes?

The bread

Skippety-Skip

We're skipping and skipping
Are Sarah and me

Skip round the playground
Skip endlessly

Skippety-skipping, mind out the way
The skippers are coming
Shout hip-hip hurray

Skippety-skippety
Skippety-skip
We're skipping and skipping
And we won't trip

Skippety-skippety
Time for a game
Let's do our favourite,
It's always the same

Johnny was a sailor
He had a little boat
He liked to eat fish fingers
But one stuck in his throat

Johnny was a sailor
He died a little death
The doctor said the cause was
A shortage of his breath

Johnny was a sailor
And he always used to shout
One two three four five six
Seven eight nine ten...OUT!

Skippety-skip, Sarah and me,
Round the playground,
Endlessly...
Endlessly...
Endlessly...

My Little Sister

My little sister's got the loudest
scream in our school. She loves

screaming

when she falls over in the playground
and hurts herself you can hear her

screaming

five whole streets away. No one
except me can get her to stop

screaming

once she's started. My dad says it
sounds like a riot. So while she's

screaming

a teacher comes to fetch me
and I have to try and stop her

screaming

I love my little sister but
I just wish sometimes she was more

quiet

Special Things

These are my special things,
I keep them just here.
There's a badge, and a shell,
And a doll with one ear;

There's a necklace that's broken,
A ring with no stone,
A pen that won't write
And an old bit of bone.

There's a dried, withered flower
My dad gave to me,
A note from my granny
And a shiny 10p.

And each of my special things
Makes me want to smile;
Each one is a memory
I can hold for a while.

These are my special things,
They'll always be near;
I'll keep them for ever...
I'll keep them just here.

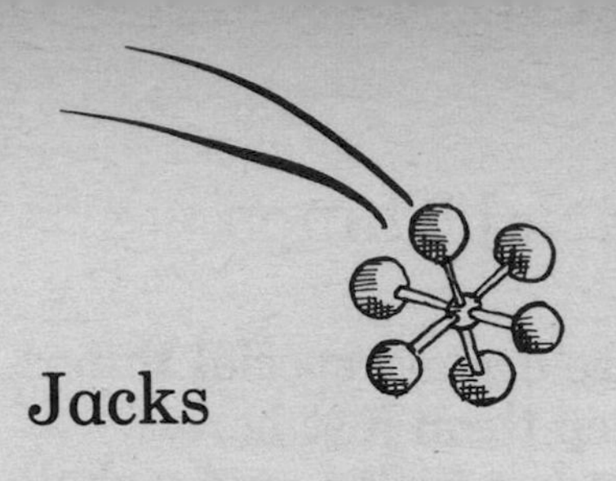

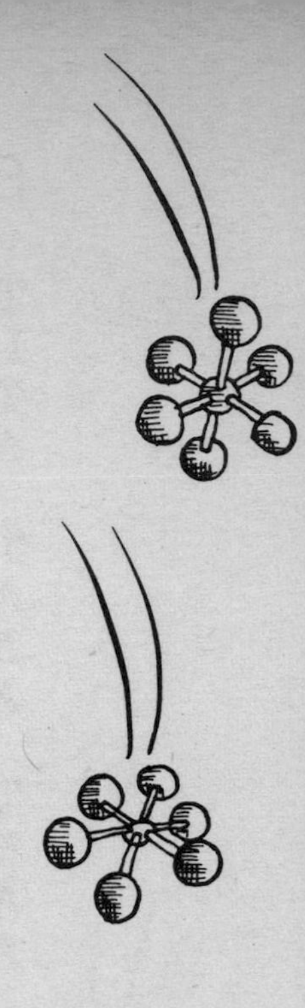

Jacks

Five silver jacks,
One rubber ball,
A playground game
For one and all.

Throw the ball,
Pick up one,
Now our game
Has just begun.

Throw the ball,
Pick up two,
One for me
And one for you.

Throw the ball,
Pick up…three!
One for you
And two for me.

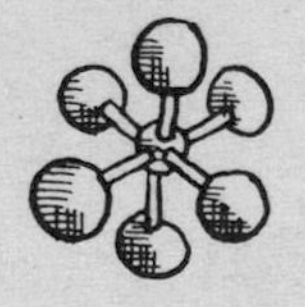

Throw the ball…
Pick up…four!
Whoops! I've dropped
One on the floor.

Throw the ball,
Here I go,
I'll try for five –
Can I? No!

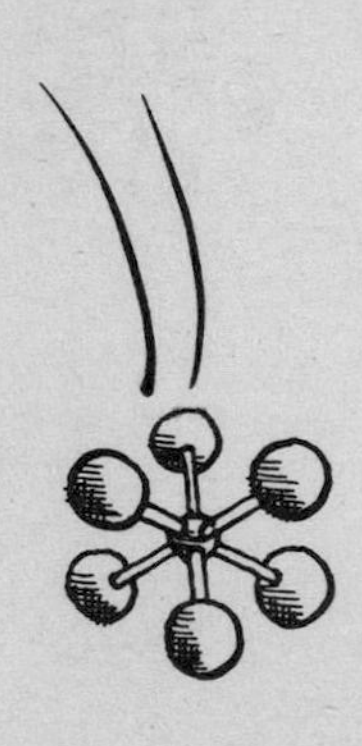

Throw the ball,
Try again…
I've got all five!
I could do TEN!

Five silver jacks,
All in a row…
Here, take the ball –
Would you like a go?

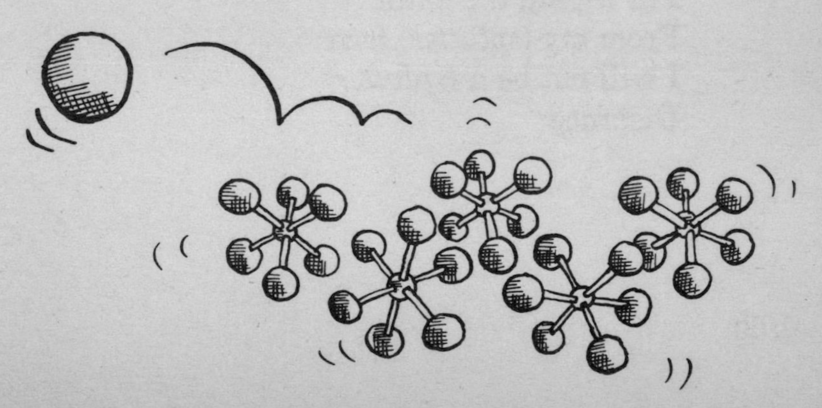

A Serious *(Giggle!)* Poem

My mum says I've got to be
Serious
In this poem

But I don't think I can I can
Feel the giggles coming on
Here they come...

My mum (*giggle*) says I'm not
(*Giggle giggle*) serious enough
Sometimes (*Giggle giggle giggle*
giggle giggle giggle giggle)

I just can't stop it, mum

Yes I can.

Right (*giggle splutter*)
I'm going to be very serious
For the rest of this po(*giggle*)em
I'm wiping the smile
From my (*splutter*) face
I will not be a (*splutter*)
Disgrace

I
Will
Not
Giggle
Mum
I
Promise

Mmmmmmmmm
(*Giggle giggle giggle*
giggle giggle giggle
giggle giggle giggle
giggle giggle giggle)
Ha Ha Giggle Giggley
Hoot Hoo Hoo Hoo

Look at my mum

She's (*giggling*) too

This is the (*splutter*)
End (*splutter*) of this
Serious (*splutter*) poem

Giggle
Giggle
Giggle

The Wobbly Wheel

This is the story
Of my friend Neil,
Who had a bike
With a wobbly wheel.

A wobbly wheel,
A wobbly wheel –
Oh, whoops! And there it goes.

Neil went racing
Down the street,
Pedalling fast
With both his feet.

Both his feet,
Both his feet –
Oh, whoops! And there they go.

The wobbly wheel
Went round and round,
When it flew off
Neil hit the ground.

Hit the ground,
Hit the ground –
Oh, whoops! And there he goes.

Then Neil got up
And with a groan
He rubbed his head
And walked off home.

Walked off home,
Walked off home –
Oh, whoops! And there he goes.

Neil had a bump
That he could feel,
So he sold his bike
With that wobbly wheel.

That wobbly wheel,
That wobbly wheel –
Oh, whoops! And there it goes.

Dressing Up

I'm a lady with a funny hat,
I'm the postman with a letter,
Now I'm a lion (or a cat),
I'm the doctor to make you better.

I'm the milkman in his float,
I'm the teacher in her class.
I'm the sail upon a boat,
I'm a bus that's whizzing past.

I'm my mother in a dress,
I'm a dancer on her toes –
And I'm doing what I like best –
Playing with my dressing-up clothes!

Pocket Money

Dad, I need some pocket money,
So can I have some – now?
I need to buy so many things,
I want some money...OWW!

Dad, you're really hurting me,
You're pulling off my ear,
And where's the money that I need?
I haven't got all year!

Dad, you're looking rather odd,
Your face has gone all red,
You're spluttering and muttering...
You should have stayed in bed.

Dad, do try to calm yourself,
You're such a wicked tease;
What's that you say? I haven't said
One simple word? Oh, *please*!

Dad, I need some pocket money,
Please...can I have some now?
But could you hurry? I must dash...
I need that money...OWWW!

Winter

It's warm by our fire,
It's cosy and nice;
My feet in their slippers,
Like two winter mice.

A drink and a biscuit,
A cuddle with dad,
A book before bedtime –
And I won't be bad.

Time for some TV,
Time for some hugs,
I'm snug as a mouse
Or a bug in a rug.

I don't mind the winter,
I don't mind the cold –
At least when I'm home
With a hot drink to hold!

Jack Frost

Jack Frost swept in
Just last night
And left the world
All wintery white.

Snowflakes swirling
All around,
Settle on houses,
Trees and ground.

Here's our snowman,
He's so fat,
He's got a scarf,
A broom and hat.

Here's a snowball,
There it goes –
Whoops! It's hit
Dad on the nose!

Let's go sliding
On a sleigh –
Look out mum,
You're in the way!

Jack Frost's lovely,
Jack Frost's nice –
And so's his world
Of snow and ice!

The Fairy

I love the fairy
On our Christmas tree,
She sits at the top
And looks down at me.

She's got a wand
And a sparkly dress,
And she's the fairy
I love the best.

Lovely fairy
On the Christmas tree,
I love you so –
Do you love me?

Morning, Yawning

In the morning
When I rise
I can't open up
My eyes

When I rise
In the morning
I can't stop myself
From yawning

When I'm yawning
I can't rise
So I think I'll
Close my eyes

Close my eyes
Goodbye morning
I'm fast asleep
I'm not yawning

Handy Dandy

Hands in mittens,
Two little kittens.

Hands in gloves,
Two cooing doves.

Hands in pockets –
I'm a rocket!

Hands in the air,
A big bad bear.

Hands like this –
Give me a kiss!

Home at Last

We struggled round shops in cold, rainy weather,
My mum and my brother and me together;
Then when we got home, we found that our dad
Had made up a fire – oh, weren't we glad!

I wriggled at bathtime right out of my clothes,
And dad put some cream on my poor, sore nose.
The water was hot, but I still felt freezing;
While mum got me dry, I couldn't stop sneezing.

I duggled down close and cuddled my mum,
She read me a story and I sucked my thumb;
Outside our house the wind howled round,
And I could hear rain splashing down on the ground.

I snuggled and duggled, deep down in my bed,
I pulled all the covers right over my head;
Outside I could hear the wild, roaring storm,
But there in my bed it was all nice and warm.